Minou

Written by Mindy Bingham

Illustrated by Itoko Maeno

Advocacy Press, Santa Barbara

Published by Advocacy Press
P.O. Box 236
Santa Barbara, California 93102

Advocacy Press is a division of the Girls Club of Santa Barbara, an affiliate of Girls Clubs of America, Inc.

GIRLS CLUBS OF AMERICA, INC.

Book design and layout by Christine Nolt

Library of Congress Cataloging-in-Publication Data
Bingham, Mindy, 1950-
Minou.
Summary: A cat who does not know how to take care of herself is abandoned in the streets of Paris and discovers self-reliance by working as a mouser at the Notre Dame Cathedral.
   [1. Cats—Fiction. 2. Paris (France)—Fiction. 3. Notre Dame de Paris (Cathedral)—Fiction. 4. Self-reliance—Fiction]
I. Maeno, Itoko, ill. II. Title.
PZ7.B511818Mi 1987 [Fic] 86-26539
ISBN 0-911655-36-0

Printed in Hong Kong

Minou was a very contented cat. She lived with her mistress, Madame Violette, on the Left Bank of the Seine River in Paris, France. Most spring mornings would find Minou lounging on their apartment balcony high above the river as the barges and the tour boats passed by below.

Life was very predictable for Minou. She and Madame Violette would get up early every morning so Madame could paint. Madame Violette was a well-known artist, and many people wanted to buy her paintings.

After lunch, Madame Violette would call
Minou and clip on her leash so they could go out
to do the daily marketing. Minou had never been
out of the apartment alone and was glad for the
security of the leash.

Some afternoons would find them visiting with the other artists in the area
as they sold their paintings along the alleys and boulevards. Minou loved the
gaiety and the hustle and bustle of the sidewalk stalls.

Other afternoons were spent in a quiet Parisian
park as Madame Violette worked for hours sketching
and painting the lovely fountains, statues, and
colorful flowers. Minou could not wander very far
on her leash, but that was all right with her because
the leash made her feel very safe and secure. It
reminded her that Madame Violette was nearby.

10

Madame Violette took very good care of Minou. She gave Minou everything a cat needs or could wish for. Minou enjoyed the care her mistress gave to her and repaid it by being cute, cuddly, and attentive. That was her whole job in life.

Of course, when someone else takes care of you, there are some things you
have to do that you don't like.

But, on the whole, Minou thought she was the luckiest cat in all of Paris.

One night Minou awoke with a start to find strangers in their home. Two
people were bending over her mistress and talking in hushed tones.

Without telling Minou why, they took Madame Violette out of the apartment on a long stretcher and quickly put her into an ambulance that hurried off into the night.

15

Poor Minou! She didn't know what had happened and she was all alone. She waited and waited for Madame Violette to return. There was no one to feed her . . .

or brush her . . .

or take her out for her walk.

16

She certainly didn't know how to feed herself, and she was getting hungry.

After three very long days, two large men finally opened the apartment door. They ignored Minou as they set to work moving Madame's furniture out to an awaiting truck. Minou heard one of them say that Madame Violette would not be coming back to the apartment because she had passed away.

"Well, what should we do about that cat?" one of the men asked as they finished moving the last piece of furniture. "The old woman did not have any relatives, so there is no one to take care of her."

"The cat will have to make it on her own," the other answered as he put Minou out, shut the front door, and drove off.

For the first time in her life, Minou was on her own.

By now, Minou was very hungry and knew she needed to find someone to take care of her. She had never taken care of herself and did not know the first thing about being on her own and independent. Without her leash, she was scared. Cautiously she set off to find a new owner.

On the Right Bank, Minou came upon a
sidewalk pet shop. There were cages filled with
cats and dogs, birds and bunnies. A man, a
woman, and a little girl were gazing into the
cages. "What luck," Minou thought, "they must
be looking for a cat to take home."

Minou scampered up to them. She rolled
onto her back on the pavement and wiggled and
played in the air with her paws, looking as cute
and cuddly as she could while the people stared
in amazement.

But just as they were about to pick her up…

...a big dog ran out of the pet shop barking and growling. Minou jumped to her feet and dashed down the boulevard. The dog chased her until he tired of the game.

By this time Minou was very, very hungry. She stopped in front of one of the many sidewalk cafés on the Avenue des Champs Élysées. Seated at gaily colored tables many people from all over the world were enjoying lively conversation, wonderful French pastries such as éclairs and croissants, and the warm spring sunshine.

One woman with a large hat caught Minou's eye. "Now if only I could get her attention," thought Minou to herself, "I know she would take me home and take care of me."

Minou knew just the way for a cat to get the attention and affection of a person.

But Minou's touch startled the lady.
She screamed and jumped to her feet.
The restaurant owner came rushing over.
He grabbed a broom and chased Minou
out of the cafe and down the boulevard.

So on Minou wandered, tired, lost and **very, very, very** hungry. Just as the shops were closing and everyone was going home for the evening, she arrived at the edge of the Place de la Concorde. The Place de la Concorde is the biggest and busiest square in Paris, with cars, trucks, and taxis rushing and honking madly. Minou had never been in such traffic before. All she knew was that she wanted to get across the street to the other side.

So she stepped off the curb....

Whish, swish went the tires of the cars. Minou darted in and out of the roaring traffic trying to avoid the cars which would not stop. Her heart pounded as one nearly ran over her.

At last she saw an opening and raced frantically to reach the other side. She ran under a bush and hid. Her eyes were wide and her fur stood on end. She felt lucky to be alive.

By now Minou was so hungry that her ribs showed. Her once beautiful fur was scruffy and matted with dirt. In fact, she was so dirty that you could not tell that she was Siamese. Minou was desperate so on she walked. She was no longer cute and cuddly, and she felt no one would want to take her home and take care of her.

Finally she sat down and cried. Minou's howling could be heard for blocks.

"Zut alors!"

Minou turned to come face to face with a sophisticated street cat who introduced herself as Celeste.

"What is all this commotion about, ma cherie! And, my word, look at you— what a sorry sight," Celeste said, shaking her head as she walked around Minou, inspecting her from whiskers to tail. "What seems to be your problem?"

Minou sadly told Celeste her story. She finished and then sobbed, "You see, there isn't anyone to take care of me anymore." Feeling sorry for herself, she went on, "I'm no longer cute and cuddly, so no one wants me."

"You know," Celeste said wisely, "not being able to take care of yourself is a very risky way to live. You can't get by on your looks alone. Everyone should know how to live alone and take care of her own needs. Come with me, and I will show you how to rely on yourself."

Celeste set to work to teach Minou how to take care of herself. Day after day Minou learned important lessons about hunting mice and finding food. Minou learned quickly and realized happily there was plenty of food if she worked for it. She did not have to worry about going hungry ever again.

Minou learned to find shelter in the nooks and crannies of the old buildings of Paris.

She even learned that giving herself a bath was much better than having someone else make her take one.

One very important lesson that Minou learned was how to cross the busy streets safely. Now she felt at home in the city without her leash. She had the confidence to go wherever she wanted.

One evening as Celeste and Minou were watching the sun set, and the sky turn many colors, Celeste turned to Minou and said, "Minou, it is time for you to find a job."

"A job!" said Minou in a startled tone. "But what can *I* do?"

"You have a lot of skills now," said Celeste. "I know of a perfect place for you, and I will take you there in the morning."

The next morning the cats were up bright and early before the streets became busy. Minou found herself following Celeste down some stairs into a long tunnel in the ground. Celeste's last lesson was how to ride the Métro, the underground train in Paris.

"Good morning, Celeste," Jacques, the conductor, said in greeting as they hopped into the cab with him. "I see you have a friend this morning. I hope you enjoy your ride."

Minou loved the fast, smooth ride. She waved her tail in thanks to Jacques when they got off the train at their station.

As they scampered out of the Métro tunnel, Minou looked upon one of the most famous churches in the world, the Notre Dame Cathedral. Minou was awed by its tremendous size and beauty. When Celeste explained that it had been built more than eight hundred years before by people without machines, trucks, or cranes, Minou could understand why it was so famous.

"Come, now—to business," said Celeste.

"The priests of the rectory need a mouser. Lately mice have been getting into the vestry and chewing holes in the beautiful, embroidered robes. Someone is needed to patrol and keep the mice out of these priceless treasures. Minou, I think you are just the cat for the job."

Before Minou could say anything, Celeste turned to leave. "I must go now, Minou. I am certain that you can now take care of yourself."

"How can I thank you?" Minou called after her.

Celeste paused, looked back over her shoulder, and in a wise and knowing tone said, "Someday you may meet another cat like you who needs someone to help her learn to live on her own. You will help that cat as I have helped you." With that she turned and walked off through the crowded square.

Minou inspected the outside of the building. As she crept along beneath the walls of the mighty cathedral she found the bell tower stairway. She raced up the 387 narrow winding steps to the roof top. What an adventure it was to explore high above the streets below!

Thousands of workers had spent years and years carving statues and gargoyles from stone to decorate the outside of the church and to carry rain water off the roof.

Once as Minou turned a corner of the building...

...one especially frightening gargoyle startled her and sent her running.

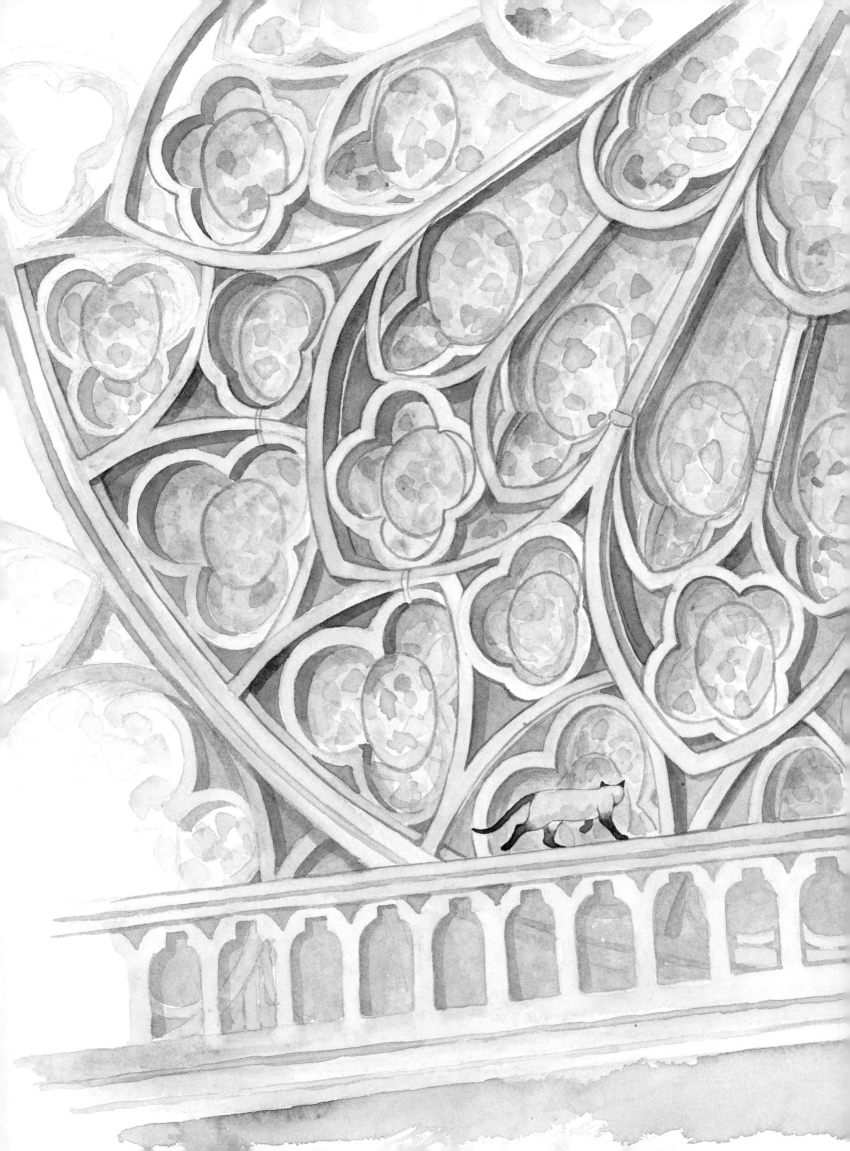

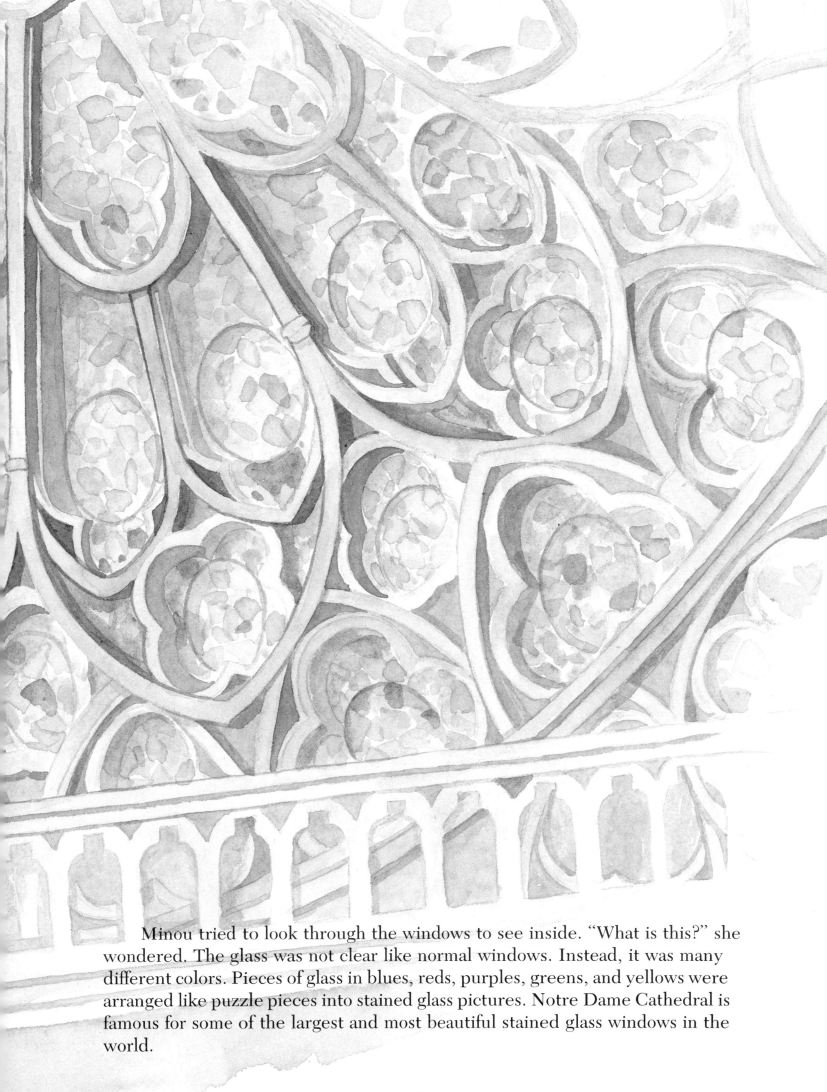

Minou tried to look through the windows to see inside. "What is this?" she wondered. The glass was not clear like normal windows. Instead, it was many different colors. Pieces of glass in blues, reds, purples, greens, and yellows were arranged like puzzle pieces into stained glass pictures. Notre Dame Cathedral is famous for some of the largest and most beautiful stained glass windows in the world.

Back on the ground, Minou scampered through the large front doors of the cathedral and stopped in astonishment.

There before her was a huge room with a ceiling so high it made her dizzy to look up at it. The ceiling was held up by the tallest stone columns she had ever seen. More than nine thousand people could come to church at one time in this large room.

Just then Minou heard a scratching sound over her shoulder. Experience told her that it was a mouse and that it was time for her to go to work.

A few minutes later, Minou proudly dropped her catch on the doorstep of the rectory, as the priests looked on.

"Père Maurice, Père Lagrange, come and see! Our prayers have been answered. We have a new mouser for the cathedral!"

They set a saucer of milk on the doorstep for Minou. She quickly lapped it up. She had not had milk for a very long time.

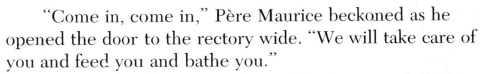

"Come in, come in," Père Maurice beckoned as he opened the door to the rectory wide. "We will take care of you and feed you and bathe you."

Minou started to step in, but suddenly stopped. "Wait a minute," she said to herself. "I don't need anyone to take care of me. I like my freedom. I will work for the priests in exchange for some milk and kindness, but I do not want anyone to own me." With that, she turned and walked off proudly with her tail straight in the air.

Today if you have a chance to visit the Notre Dame Cathedral in Paris, you might see Minou. During the day she can be found either basking in the sun high above the city or posing for a tourist's photograph in the garden behind the cathedral.

You might find her joining one of the many daily tours of the beautiful church and listening to the guide tell about the building's history.

Minou knows that, if she ever wants milk, all she has to do is go to work for the priests.

Every once in awhile, Celeste comes to visit Minou. Celeste is very pleased
to see how happy Minou is in her new life. Minou is her own mistress now and
knows how to take care of herself.

Every evening as the sun is setting and the lights
of Paris are turning the dusk into a twinkle, Minou can be
seen crossing the bridge to the Île Saint Louis—to no one
knows where.
    Minou is
        ...a cat of independent means!

Minou's Sites of Paris

Page 4-5 **The Seine River** This river divides Paris into the *Right Bank* (fashionable hotels, shops, and great boulevards) and the *Left Bank* (the Latin Quarter, Sorbonne, the center of artistic and intellectual activity).

Page 20-21 **Palais de Justice** Among this complete block of buildings is the infamous prison of the Conciergerie, where Marie Antoinette and other victims of the French Revolution awaited the guillotine, and the beautiful Gothic Church of Sainte-Chapelle. **Pont Neuf** The bridge in the background is the oldest bridge in Paris, dating back to the seventeenth century.

Page 24-25 **Arc de Triomphe** Commissioned by Napoleon Bonaparte in 1806, this is the largest triumphal arch in the world. The view of Paris from the top is magnificent. **Champs-Élysées** This wide and elegant boulevard is famous for its outdoor cafés, fashionable shops and luxurious apartment houses.

Page 28-29 **Place de la Concorde** The site of the guillotine during the French Revolution, this magnificent square with its lovely statues and fountains offers sweeping vistas from all directions. The special lighting at night gives it a magical quality.

Page 32-33 **Jardin des Tuileries** These seventeenth-century formal gardens are a popular respite for Parisians and tourists. Children enjoy sailing boats in the large octagonal pool.

Page 35 **The Louvre** This is the largest museum in the world. It houses some of the greatest art treasures of all time, including the *Winged Victory, Venus de Milo*, and the *Mona Lisa.*

Page 38-39 **L'Opéra** The largest theater in the world, this ornate showplace is a symbol of lavish luxury and splendor.

Page 40-41 **Pont Alexandre III** Built in 1900, this is the most magnificent and ornate bridge in Paris. **Eiffel Tower** This ingenious iron structure, dedicated in 1889, has become the symbol of Paris.

Page 42 **Entrance to the Métro** Opened in 1900, the Paris Métro is a very efficient and easy-to-understand mode of transportation. The ornate Métro entrances of art nouveau baldachins and flower motifs are a cherished Parisian sight.

Page 44-45 **Notre Dame de Paris** Started in 1163, this church is one of the finest examples of Gothic architecture in the world. Notre Dame is especially famous for its stained glass windows, sculpture, gargoyles, vaulted ceilings and flying buttresses.

Page 57 **Northern Rose Window** This masterpiece still retains the thirteenth-century glass.

Page 60-61 **View of Notre Dame Cathedral from the Île Saint Louis** One of the most attractive parts of Paris, the serene Île Saint Louis has magnificent old mansions dating from the seventeenth century.

About the Author:

Since 1973 Mindy Bingham has been the Executive Director of the Girls Club of Santa Barbara, California. Coauthor of four other books including the best seller: *CHOICES: A Teen Woman's Journal for Self-awareness and Personal Planning*, she is especially interested in writing on equity issues for girls and young women.

A sought-after speaker and trainer on early equity issues for school districts around the country, she was named one of the Outstanding Women in Education in Santa Barbara County in 1985. She lives with her daughter Wendy in Santa Barbara.

About the Illustrator:

Itoko Maeno was born in Tokyo, where she studied at Tama Art University. She came to the United States in 1982. Since then, her art has appeared in many books including *CHOICES: A Teen Woman's Journal for Self-awareness and Personal Planning.*

Itoko is accomplished in a wide range of styles but she is best known for her delicate and intricate water colors. When not working on illustration, she creates fine art in ceramics and through abstract expressionist painting of landscapes and flowers.

Itoko worked for nearly a year on the Minou illustrations. The final product radiates her love and understanding of Paris, cats and art.

It doesn't matter where a girl comes from, as long as she knows where she's going.
Girls Clubs of America's Motto

Society still tells girls they have a choice as to whether or not they will work for pay. Yet:

- Women are nine times as likely as men to be single parents.

- 90% of today's girls will work for pay at some time in their lives.

- Over 50% of today's girls will probably support families on their own at some time in their lives.

- 93% of AFDC (welfare) dollars support families headed by women.

- 70% of the elderly poor are women.

The beliefs and attitudes of both girls and boys will need to change if they are to be prepared for the new realities of paid work and family roles. With the following suggestions you can act privately and publicly to reduce or eliminate societal barriers to girls' achievement.

Introduce girls to women and men in the world of work in both traditional and nontraditional jobs.

Use the language of skill and success to compliment girls.

Encourage and praise risk-taking in girls and care-taking in boys.

Avoid rescuing girls. Help them become problem solvers.

Watch your language: Watch other people's. Don't talk in sex stereotypes. Use gender-neutral labels.

Make high technology relevant and accessible to girls.

Read what children are reading. Point out sexist messages/advertising. Write protest letters together.

Watch TV with children; help them analyze what they are seeing.

Try some role reversals at home. Let Dad do the dishes; son bathe the baby; daughter mow the lawn or take out the garbage.

Encourage math competency and mastery in girls. Point out future career benefits.

Sustain high aspirations in early adolescence.

Encourage self-sufficiency by continuously questioning and prodding children to expand their options.

You might ask these questions:

Why couldn't Minou take care of herself in the beginning of the story?

When Minou lived with Madame Violette, what was her job?

Do you think Minou ever thought she would have to take care of herself?

How might Minou have been better prepared to take care of herself when she was on her own in Paris?

Will someone take care of you when you are grown up?

What is the best way to prepare for a good job so you can take care of yourself?

What jobs do you think you might like to do when you grow up?

Girls Clubs of America, Inc., An Action Agenda for Equalizing Girls' Options and
Facts and Reflections on Careers for Today's Girls (New York, 1985).

Other books by Advocacy Press:

Choices: A Teen Woman's Journal for Self-awareness and Personal Planning, by Mindy Bingham, Judy Edmondson and Sandy Stryker. Softcover, 240 pages. ISBN 0-911655-22-0.

Challenges: A Young Man's Journal for Self-awareness and Personal Planning, by Bingham, Edmondson and Stryker. Softcover, 240 pages. ISBN 0-911655-24-7.

Gifts every parent, grandparent and caring adult will want to give the teenagers in their lives. CHOICES and CHALLENGES engagingly address the myths and hard realities each teenager will face in entering adulthood. They contain thought-provoking exercises that prompt young people to think about their futures, develop quantitative goals, make sound decisions, assert themselves, and evaluate career options, marriage, child-rearing responsibilities and lifestyle budgeting.

Father Gander Nursery Rhymes: The Equal Rhymes Amendment, by Father Gander. Hardcover with dust jacket, full color illustrations throughout, 48 pages, ISBN 0-911655-12-3.

Without losing the charm, whimsy and melody of the original *Mother Goose* rhymes, each of Father Gander's delightful rhymes provides a positive message in which both sexes, all races and ages and people with a myriad of handicaps interact naturally and successfully.

You can find these books at better bookstores. Or you may order them directly by sending $14.45 each (includes shipping) to Advocacy Press, P.O. Box 236, Dept. A, Santa Barbara, California 93102. For your review we will be happy to send you more information on these publications.